Madam Hortensia

Text © 2020 Carmen Gil

Illustrations © 2020 Miguel Cerro

© 2020 Cuento de Luz SL

Calle Claveles, 10 | Pozuelo de Alarcón | 28223 | Madrid | Spain

www.cuentodeluz.com

Original title in Spanish: *Doña Hortensia*

English translation by Jon Brokenbrow

ISBN: 978-84-18302-13-8

Printed in PRC by Shanghai Cheng Printing Company July 2020,
print number 1815-7

CUENTO
DE LUZ

STONE
PAPER®
NO TREES - NO WATER - NO BLEACH

This book is printed on **Stone Paper©** that is Silver **Cradle to Cradle™** certified.

Cradle to Cradle™ is one of the most demanding ecological certification systems, awarded to products that have been conceived and designed in an ecologically intelligent way.

Certified
B
Corporation®

Cuento de Luz™ became a **Certified B Corporation©** in 2015. The prestigious certification is awarded to companies which use the power of business to solve social and environmental problems and meet higher standards of social and environmental performance, transparency, and accountability.

Madam Hortensia

Carmen Gil
Miguel Cerro

Madam Hortensia loved straight lines. She absolutely hated wavy lines, zig-zags, and curves.

That's why she had a garden full of daisies arranged in perfectly straight lines. Each one was in exactly the right place.

All of the paintings in her living room were hung at the same height.

None of them were any higher, or any lower than another.

Her alarm clock rang every day at exactly 7:18.

Not one minute before, or one minute after.

Every morning, Madam Hortensia would prepare a mixture of honey and seeds, and spread it onto four identical pieces of toast. None of them were any larger, or any smaller than another.

When she finished, she would take out her dog, Starchy, and they would walk as far as the fifth pine tree.

Not one tree nearer, or one tree farther.

Then she would walk to the bus stop, catch the
number 22 to the park, and sit in seat number 33.

Not one seat closer to the back, or closer to the front.

When she arrived at the park, she would feed eight ducks, three pheasants, and two peacocks.

Not one bird more, or one bird less.

Once she returned home, she would listen to the same program on the radio, listening to people whose thoughts were just like hers.

They didn't move their ideas one inch to one side or one inch to the other side.

At night, Madam Hortensia went to bed exactly when the first ray of moonlight shone through her window.

Not one moment before, or one moment after.

And so, Madam Hortensia did exactly the same thing every day of the week, every week of the month, and every month of the year.

If someone asked her, "Why don't you do something different?"

She'd say, "Why change things, when they're perfectly fine?"

But one morning, something astonishing happened. The alarm clock didn't go off on time. It rang at 7:32! Madam Hortensia didn't have time to prepare her usual breakfast.

"What a catastrophe!" she complained.

So she had no choice other than to eat the blueberry jelly she'd been given as a present.

"Mmmmm . . . delicious!" she said as she tasted it.

She did not have time to walk as far as the fifth pine tree with her dog, Starchy.

"What a disaster!" she sighed.

So she took him to the dog park on the corner.

There, Starchy met a friendly pup who made him wag his tail and jump for joy.

"Woof, woof, woof!" he barked.

Later, even though she rushed to the bus stop, Madam Hortensia missed the number 22 bus.

"What a tragedy!" she said.

And so, for the first time in her life, she rented a bicycle.

"Goodness me! All this pedaling is absolutely wonderful!" she admitted.

She enjoyed herself so much, that by the time she arrived at the park, the gate was locked.

"What a calamity!" she grumbled.

But since she was there, she decided to look around at the kite display in front of the park. There were kites in the shape of butterflies, flowers, jellyfish, and dragons. While she was there, she made one for herself that was like a beautiful, brightly-colored bird. On the way home, she stopped in a field to fly it.

"Heavens above, this really is fun!" she said.

She had so much fun with her kite, the time just flew by. When she arrived home, her favorite radio program had ended.

"What a tragedy!" she complained.

Madam Hortensia had to find another station. The people who were talking had different ideas from her own, and they made her see a different point of view.

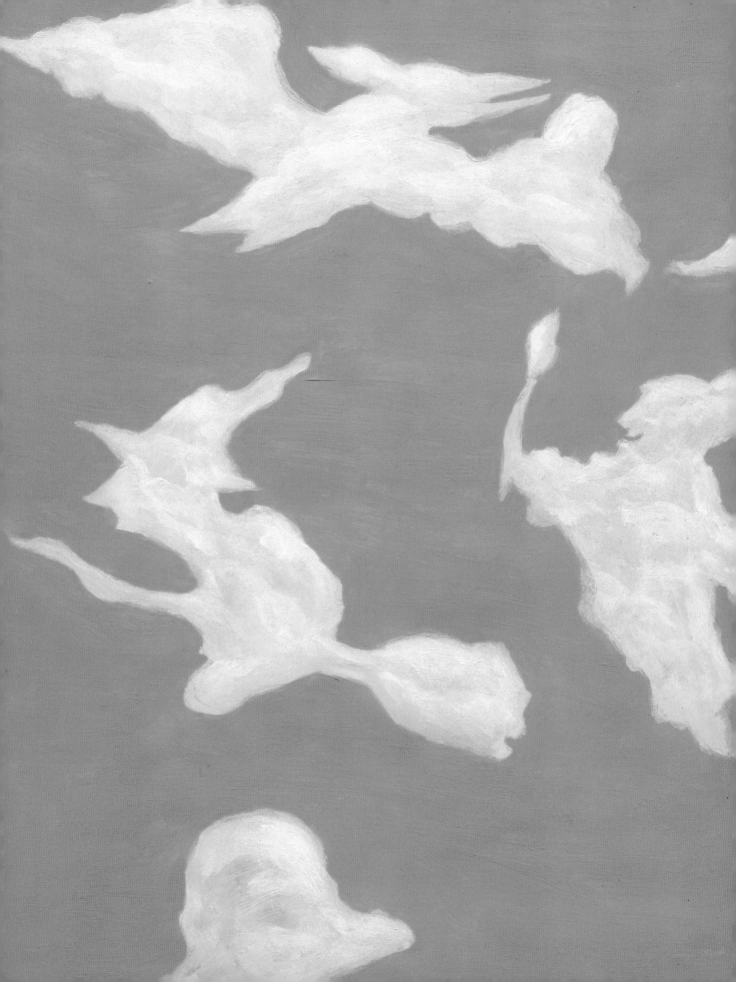

"My word! I'd always thought that clouds were just clouds, and now it turns out they can be flying dinosaurs, or witches on broomsticks, or spaceships!"

Madam Hortensia sat down to draw them, until it was very late. So late, in fact, that she couldn't go to sleep with the first ray of moonlight.

"What a disaster!" she said.

She looked out the window and saw a swarm of fireflies floating in the night sky.

"The night is so beautiful!" she thought to herself.

And she went to bed with her heart full of joy.

So from the day her alarm clock failed to wake her on time, Madam Hortensia came to love wavy lines like the sea along the shore; curves like Mr. Gordon's lips, that were always smiling; and zig-zags, like the fluttering flight of the bats outside her window.

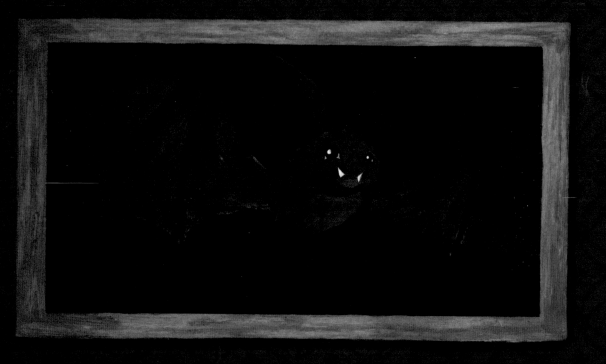

Sometimes people would ask her, "Why don't you do the same thing every day of the week, every week of the month, and every month of the year, like you used to?"

She would always reply, "Because things that are just fine can get even better. All you've got to do is give them a chance. Nothing more, and nothing less!"

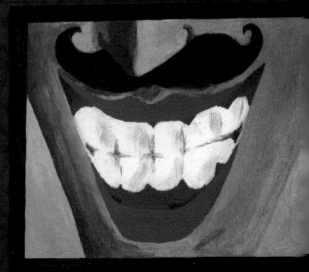